To Simon and Chloë

for all the sandcastles you have built

and the holes you have dug.

British Library Cataloguing in Publication Data
A catalogue record for this book is available from the British Library.

ISBN 0 340 75266 1 Hardback
ISBN 0 340 75267 X Paperback

10 9 8 7 6 5 4 3 2 1

First published 2000
by Hodder Children's Books
a division of Hodder Headline Limited
338 Euston Road London NW1 3BH

Printed in Hong Kong

HARRIET ADRIFT

DEBORAH INKPEN

A division of Hodder Headline Limited

The sky was the colour of Emily's dress. A clear brilliant blue. Summer had arrived and Emily and Billy were visiting Aunt Lucy.

The cases were packed. The sun hats were packed. Even Harriet was packed.

Emily had insisted.

Aunt Lucy lived by the sea. She had a beach hut. Number 22.

It was painted yellow, green, red and blue.

The sun came up. The hats came out. Everyone was off to the beach.

But Emily was watching Harriet.

'Come on, Emily,' said Billy.

Emily hesitated.

Then she opened the cage, picked up the little hamster and popped her into her pocket.

'You can come too,' she said.

Down on the beach they all bundled into the beach hut, shedding shirts, shorts, socks and shoes, and squeezing themselves into swimsuits.

Emily threw down her jumper, and only just remembered Harriet.

Billy grabbed his boat. Emily picked up her bucket. She put Harriet inside and set off along the beach.

Harriet joggled along uncomfortably. She peeped out over the rim. A small shell landed on her head. Then a large lump of seaweed.

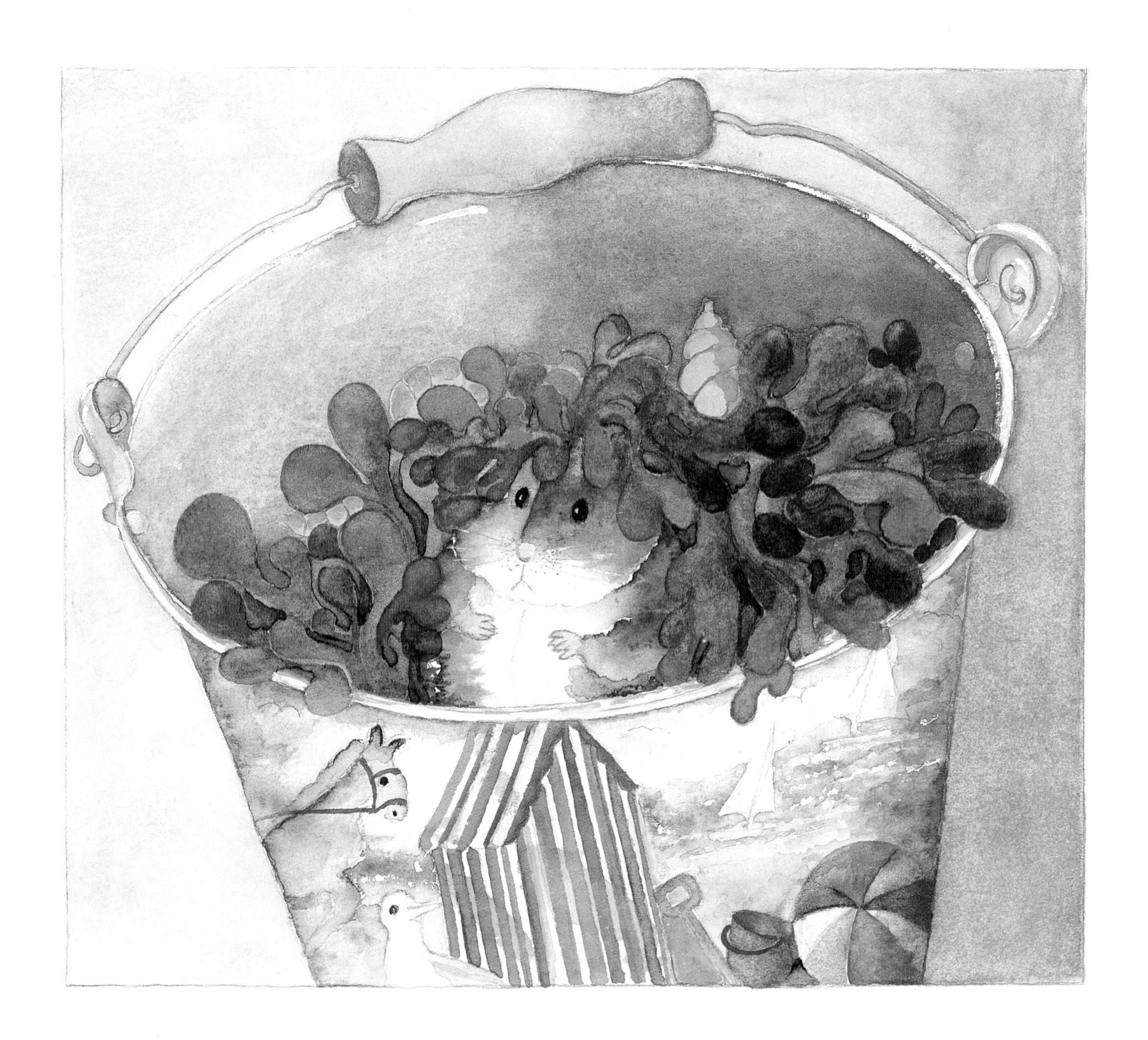

Emily wandered back with her bucket of treasures. She sat down and began to make a sandcastle. Billy asked if she'd seen his boat. Emily shook her head and carried on with her castle.

When she had finished she placed a shell and her best bit of seaweed on the top. She added Harriet.

'You're the King of the Castle,' she sang.

Just then Aunt Lucy called out,
'Ice-cream, Emily!' And Emily ran off.

Harriet climbed carefully down from her castle.

Harriet picked her way around the slippery rocks that lay along the shore. She hadn't gone very far when she came across a rather odd-looking one.

It had two tiny eyes and big, snapping claws.

Harriet backed away.

The rock side-stepped closer.

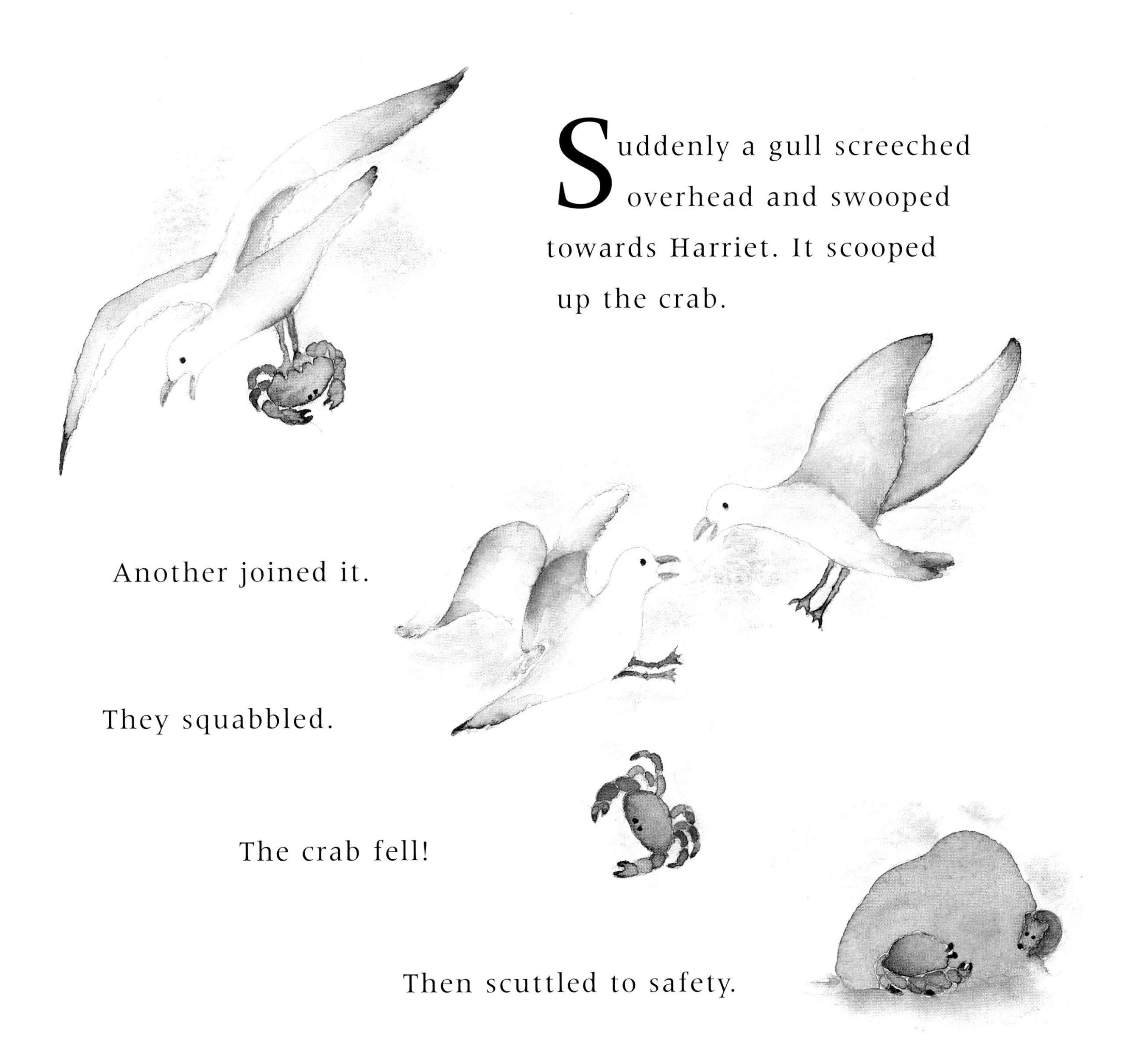

Suddenly a gull screeched overhead and swooped towards Harriet. It scooped up the crab.

Another joined it.

They squabbled.

The crab fell!

Then scuttled to safety.

A ribbon of silver water sparkled its way out to sea and there, resting against its bank, was Billy's little boat.

Curious, Harriet approached. The boat rocked gently as she nosed her way aboard.

A small breeze caught the sails. The boat began to move, slowly at first; then, drifting with the tide, it made its way steadily upstream.

Harriet looked out. She was surrounded by water.

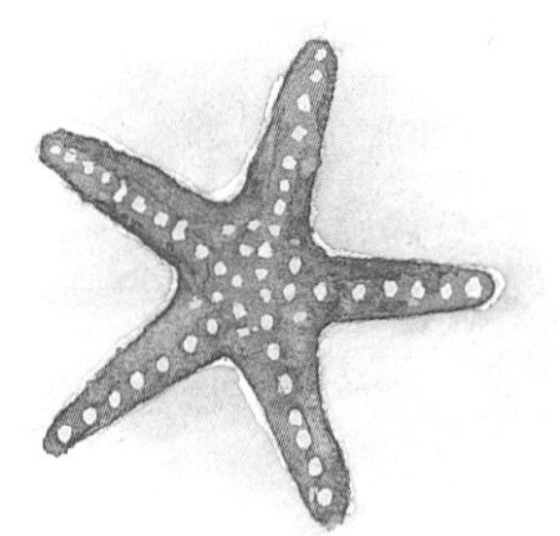

The little boat gathered speed and Harriet found herself sailing into a small rock pool.

She peered over the side. Shadows darted through the water and strange blobs of jelly waved feathery fingers.

A sudden gust of wind sent the boat spinning round the pool. Harriet felt quite dizzy.

The wind dropped and the current pushed the little boat upstream once more.

The boat sailed lazily on.

Soon dark clouds began to gather. The sun disappeared and the breeze became stronger. Waves began to toss the little boat from side to side and salty water splashed over Harriet.

She climbed to the top of the mast, clinging on tightly.

Overhead she heard the screech of the gulls.

Big drops of rain fell on Emily as she ran back to her castle.

Harriet had gone.

The tide was coming in. Water poured into the little streams and inlets along the sand and the beach began to look unfamiliar.

Emily searched frantically. She looked under the shells. She looked under the seaweed. She looked in her bucket. Harriet was nowhere to be seen.

A tear ran down Emily's face as the first wave lapped her sandcastle.

Then suddenly Billy shouted, 'There's my boat!'

The tide had brought Billy's boat back and clinging to its mast was Emily's little hamster.

'Emily, what is Harriet doing in my boat?'

Emily just beamed at Billy.

'She's on holiday too,' said Emily.

Back at the beach hut they huddled from the rain. Aunt Lucy gave them strawberries.

'I like your beach hut, Aunt Lucy,' said Emily, feeding her hamster another strawberry.
'And so does Harriet.'